A Note for Parents and Teachers

A focus on phonics
helps beginning readers gain
skill and confidence with reading.
Each story in the Bright Owl Books series
highlights one vowel sound—for *Go Home, Goat*, it's the
long "o" sound. At the end of the book, you'll find three
Story Starters, just for fun. Story Starters are open-ended
questions that can be used as a jumping-off place for
conversation, storytelling, and imaginative writing.

At Kane Press, we believe the most important part
of any reading program is the shared experience
of a good story. We hope you'll enjoy
Go Home, Goat with a child you love!

For all bright-eyed, bright owl readers.

Library of Congress Cataloging-in-Publication Data
Names: Coxe, Molly, author, illustrator.
Title: Go home, Goat / by Molly Coxe.
Description: New York : Kane Press, [2019] | Series: Bright Owl books |
Summary: One cold, snowy day Goat asks Mole, Snowshoe Hare, and Polar Bear if he can warm up in their homes, because he has no home of his own.
Identifiers: LCCN 2018024731| ISBN 9781635921014 (pbk) | ISBN 9781635921007 (reinforced library binding) | ISBN 9781635921021 (ebook)
Subjects: | CYAC: Cold—Fiction. | Home—Fiction. | Friendship—Fiction. | Goats—Fiction. | Animals—Fiction.
Classification: LCC PZ7.C839424 Go 2019 | DDC [E]—dc23
LC record available at https://lccn.loc.gov/2018024731

10 9 8 7 6 5 4 3 2 1

First published in the United States of America in 2019 by Kane Press, Inc.
Printed in China

Book Design: Michelle Martinez

Bright Owl Books is a registered trademark of Kane Press, Inc.

Visit us online at www.kanepress.com

 Like us on Facebook
facebook.com/kanepress

 Follow us on Twitter
@KanePress

GO HOME, GOAT

by Molly Coxe

Kane Press • New York

Snow. Snow. Snow.
"Brrrrrrrrr," says Goat.
"My nose is cold.
So are my toes!"

"Can I come in, Mole?"

"No," says Mole.
"My hole is full of snow.
Go home, Goat!"

Blow. Blow. Blow.
"Brrr," says Goat.
"My nose is cold.
So are my toes!"

"Can I come in,
Snowshoe Hare?"

"No," says Snowshoe Hare.
"Our burrow can't hold a goat.
Go home, Goat!"

Roam. Roam. Roam.
"Brrrr," says Goat.
"My nose is cold.
So are my toes."

"Can I come in,
Polar Bear?"

"No," says Polar Bear.
"You broke my pole.
Go home, Goat!"

21

"I don't have a home,"
 says Goat.
"Oh!" says Polar Bear.
"I didn't know."

And a cozy coat!

"Don't go!" says Goat.
"Stay and have some oats!"

Everyone has oats.
Then they make a snowgoat.
Its nose is cold.
So are its toes.

But not Goat.
He is toasty
inside his new home.

Glow. Glow. Glow.
"I love my home," says Goat.

Story Starters

Who is in the hole?

Polar Bear and Mole
have a globe.
Where will they go?

The snow bunnies
are two days old.
What will Goat show them?